The Gay Icon
Contemporary Short
Stories
Robert Joseph Greene

ICON EMPIRE PRESS
Toronto Vancouver New York London
The Gay Icon
Contemporary Short
Stories
ISBN 9780986929762

No part of this ebook may be reproduced or transmitted in any form or by any means, graphic, electronic, or mechanical, including photocopying, recording, taping, or by any information storage retrieval system, without the permission in writing from the publisher.

published by ICON EMPIRE PRESS 552 Church Street Toronto, ON M4Y 2E3 CANADA.

NOTICE

All characters appearing in this work are fictitious. Any resemblance to any real persons, living or dead, is purely coincidental.

ACKNOWLEDGEMENT

I would like to thank Camilla Greene, Thomas Greene, Kelli-Anne, Caleb Greene, Stanley Bennett Clay, Bonnie Yiu, Bobby Nijjar, Dan Mohan, John Weger, Stephanie Yuen, Mairi Welman, Tim Tewsley, Peter Jones, Derek Hewlett, Dan Di Luigi, Karol Sienkiewicz, Colin Clode, Genevieve Iacovino, Ben Besler for their proofreading and editing and/or moral support.

TABLE OF CONTENTS

The Gay Icon Contemporary Short Stories

INTRODUCTION
I think my introduction will be just as enlightening as these short stories. Once I read The Affairs of the Heart (Amores), which was attributed to an Assyrian rhetorician called Lucian of Samosata (c. A.D. 125 – after A.D. 180).
The subject matter of The Affairs of the Heart (Amores) would be shocking to today's society and therefore I will circumvent the details, and place more general terms on this great piece of literature.

The writings (Amores) tell of a great debate concerning whether the love of a male or female is better, from a man's perspective. I found that both arguments were very strong and compelling. I also felt that the conclusions were weak. They concluded that for the purposes of procreation the love of a woman would have to win. We now live in an overpopulated earth. I see no reason to justify institutionalizing procreation, let alone using it as a plausible reason for loving someone. What was also said in Amores was that the love shared between men had a special virtue that did not exist in women. I believe (whether gay or straight) love is equal. However, it wasn't until recently that gay love was expressed in fiction. The short stories you are about to read will always have a heroic measure of virtue in them. Even in tragedy a lesson is learned in the affairs of the heart.

-Robert Joseph Greene

The Difference between Buddies and Lovers

What I wanted to do was run after him. I wanted to say, "Wait. Look. He was just showing me his tattoo." But these were just afterthoughts. Michael had opened the door to the shed at the moment we were scrambling, fastening our pants and tucking in our shirts. It was only moments before we heard them.

"I think I have the bag in here," I heard Michael say to some unknown guests as he opened the shed door. This is where my partner found me with Adam. Adam and I quickly pulled away from each other, pulling up our pants. We were almost in the clear, but we weren't fast enough. Michael had opened the door. The light flowing upon the dark cramped corners of the shed rendered our verdict: guilty.

Our eyes met for a second, but it seemed like an eternity. Michael didn't even look to see who was beside me. I glanced over Michael's shoulder and saw that the guests weren't looking in the shed, but were admiring the flowers Michael had so proudly planted in our garden earlier this spring. His garden. At least, we didn't have any further embarrassment, or witnesses. Michael quickly shut the shed door, turning to the outside guests, saying that the flower fertilizer is probably in the garage and not the shed. His voice quivered with hurt as he explained this, a hurt that was only known to me, and not our unsuspecting guests.

I go over that day in my head like it was yesterday. Instead of imagining not ever venturing into the shed with young Adam, I envision scenarios of acceptable excuses that would have kept Michael and I together.

God, how I loved (and still love) Michael. How I ruined a perfectly happy moment in my life. I had been with Michael for two years. It wasn't perfect but it was stable and safe. In hindsight, I was happy. It was seconds after the shed closed that I realized how content my life was, and that it was all over. I guess I have always been the type of person who recognized happiness only after it's passed.

"Hey buddy, we better get out of here," said Adam. I wasn't sure if he meant to go somewhere more discreet to finish what we had started, or just to drop the whole thing. Adam was the only guest that I invited. He and I had a class at the local community college. Michael was paying for me to go. He felt that I should have direction in life. I just went with the program laid out for me by Michael. I hate school.

Adam was just about my physical ideal. He was fit, young, and played it straight. He was more muscular and masculine than Michael. However, Michael had friendliness about him whereas Adam seemed more selfish.

Adam called everyone 'buddy.' He forgot names easily and that was his way of disguising the fact. In class, Adam often caught me gazing upon him. We talked a little during the days but nothing deep. Nothing like the three hour conversation Michael and I had when we first met. I decided to invite Adam to a cocktail party that Michael and I were having. I should have clued in about Adam when he arrived with Corona that this wasn't his sort of party. "Hey buddy!" he said loudly as he handed me two six packs at our door.

I lost Michael that night. After the incident, he was so gracious at the party, whereas I was a mess inside. For the rest of that night, we played the part of a happy couple, but the strain was evident. When couples were around us, I would move closer to touch him, but he kindly found some reason to move away from me. I wanted the party to be over so that we could quit this charade. I started drinking heavily to dull my pain. Michael was obviously trying to keep busy and stay involved in every conversation of our guests. His guests. The people he invited were a sophisticated, pseudo-intellectual collection of refined queers who had nothing better to do with their lives but redecorate their homes, go to movies and host multi-flavored martini parties.

If ever I had a wish in my entire life, it would be to meet Michael. Today. Sure, he'd be much older. He was 16 years older than me. It has been several years since the incident, since we last saw each other. Sure, I would run into Michael a couple of times after at parties, but he would never really talk to me the way he did before. What we shared was gone, in his mind.

I remember being so drunk by the time Myna, the last guest, left. I panicked and grabbed her, asking her to stay just a few minutes longer. Michael reassuringly took our stunned captive from my embrace, and said that he was sure it was late for her. She said her goodbyes.

I went to find Michael. I wanted to hold him. I wanted to console him. But he just pushed me away. Frustrated, and in a drunken stupor, I wrestled him to the floor. I pinned him down. I was much more powerful than he. He lay there helpless. "I will kill you if you make me leave," I said as the tears blurred my vision. I never really meant to be so drastic. As I gazed down upon his saddened figure, I thought him to be the most handsome man ever.

He calmly said the most piercing words, "And I am guilty of this second death that you will bestow upon me for what reason?" I didn't understand his fancy talk, but there was no missing the message in his eyes. They were saying, "Such beauty was not worth such pain." He remained cold and emotionless under my weight on the cold floor.

I released my hold on him, got up, and stumbled towards the guest room. Moments later, Michael came into the room with my backpack. "I've booked you a week at the motel on Highway 17-92." I expected him to do that. I had only hoped he would have waited until morning.

Eventually, I moved in with a couple of friends in the neighboring town. Adam and I had only seen each other a few times after. There was no real connection there. He was really a casual sex sort of guy, and didn't have any intentions of us growing into something more. I began to despise his, "Hey buddy," openers every time we met. Perhaps, it reminded me that we were one in the same. There was our kind, and then there were the type of gay men like Michael. I came to realize that there are horndogs and there are believers. Horndogs can only be with buddies, not lovers. Even when we have a lover, all we see is a buddy.

Michael, as I later learned, was a rare breed of gay man. He was a believer. He wasn't sarcastic, insecure, or bitter about anything in gay life. Even at his age, he still believed in love, even though guys all around him were growing bitter and tired of the game. In looking back on it all, Michael really made an effort to make his home our home. He tolerated my youthful brashness and ignorance in life and relationships. He weathered my emotional ups and downs. Me, I was young, but told myself I knew it all. I looked upon our being together as an opportunity, and not as an existence.

I have never been one to analyze things. But if I was to look at my actions, and myself, I would see that I was (and possibly still am) a horndog. I don't have to tell you that. You just read it. And if I were to be really truthful, I have always been that way.

I remember it wasn't too long before meeting Michael that I was giving blow jobs for beer money. I was cute. I was young. These things were recipes for success in gay life. As I got my twenty dollars from these men, I'd always say, "Thanks buddy," as if I were surprised they gave it to me. No one ever knew about the beer money work, except for those 4 or 5 "buddies."

Love doesn't mean anything to me, but I wish it did. Some horndog types would say love matters, but they'd be lying to themselves. We'd be lying to ourselves. And there lies the difference between believers and horndogs, lovers and buddies, Michael and Myself. To Michael, we were lovers. To me, we were buddies. The difference between he and I is that he really cared about us and I didn't. If I did, I would be fantasying about being faithful to Michael instead of thinking of plausible excuses that would have made the moment right and kept us together. And the difference between the two fantasies is that the first would have made two of us happy, and not just me.

The Stones on the Floor

"All, all, all in together wow,
How do you like the weather
now?
January, February, March…"
And that is how my sister and her
friends skipped rope. Singing.
"You comin?" Darnell yelled as
he was running to the court to
play some ball.
"You know I can't, stupid," I
replied.
Gone are the lazy summer days
when I could play some
basketball and hang out with the
gang. I'm not trying to make you
sad. It's just the way it is.
It was no surprise that dad died.
Trying to keep up with the busy

pace of running his own restaurant, and having a night job to meet those heavy loan payments at the end of every month. He was trying to make life better for his family. Some life, I thought. He died and I had to drop out of school and work beside momma at the restaurant. Momma and I worked day and night, cooking, cleaning and serving food in the only black soul food restaurant in town.

I wasn't a good cashier or waiter. Momma said I gave too much attitude and didn't smile.

Fuck that shit!

Momma would often have to come out from the kitchen and say a nice hello, just so somebody would give a smile to the customers. She knew I hated it here.

Darnell appeared at the back door of the restaurant. It had been several months since I hung out with the crew. The crew was us fellas. We hung around in one big group. Darnell acted like our leader and shit. He and I were the oldest. In summer, we'd fished, drank, and partied, but that was last year. This year is different. Darnell and I were tight, like brothers.

Darnell seemed bored but he didn't admit it. He arrived at the time that the miller arrived with the heavy loads of flour for momma's baking. Darnell saw me carry the one hundred pound bags of flour. I nearly dropped 'em.

They were fucking heavy bags. It was Darnell who insisted that he carry the bags of flour.

"Get your chump ass off those bags, Mutha fucka!"

"Yeah, you and what army is gonna stop me?"

It was dumb but I dared Darnell to see who could run faster with a load of flour. I pointed to a tree that was maybe a hundred yards away. We grabbed our bags of flour and ran. It was really stupid. We both started to laugh half-way. Darnell won.

I was really tired after all that running but I didn't admit it. I tripped and dropped my bag of flour. It broke open, spraying both of us. We looked all white faced and shit. At first we were laughing real hard, but Momma came out and yelled at us.

I felt bad because she now had to pay for useless flour which was yet another financial setback. Darnell felt worse. Every day after that, he was at our restaurant carrying shit and picking up things for us. Sure enough, with each and every delivery at the restaurant, Darnell was there to pick up the order and place it in our storage cellar or cooler. At first, momma told him that we had no money for extra help but he kept at it.

This went on almost all summer. Darnell started coming in the mornings and leaving around lunchtime. Momma felt bad because we couldn't pay him. She even offered him lunch, but Darnell refused.

Summer was just about over, when one night Darnell threw stones at my window. Times were tough for us. So we sold our home and moved into the apartment above the restaurant. It was hot that night and my window was wide open. So, the stones just hit the floor. A stone hit my foot on the bed and I woke up. Everyone was asleep. I looked out my window and saw Darnell. I came down in my boxers and a t-shirt that I slept in.

"Wut up?"

"Let's go to Watkins Lake."

I was about to go inside to get a towel, but Darnell stopped me. He had two towels on him.

Darnell also had a six-pack of Schlitz Malt Liquor. He definitely stole that shit from his dad. As we were walking, the trees were so far apart it didn't seem like real woods. We were drinking and talking like the summer before my dad died.

The moon was glowing on that clear night. I tried keeping a look out for poison ivy but it was too dark to see. I tripped over a branch and cursed. Darnell grabbed my arm so that I wouldn't fall. I guess I was getting drunk.

We got farther along towards the lake, and the ground tilted down at an angle. It was difficult walking, but I was able to balance. Darnell wasn't so lucky.

He was having trouble walking and carrying the cans of Schlitz, towels and all.

"Darnell, buddy, give me some of that." He is stubborn and refuses. "Fuck this shit, next time we're taking the path."

I saw the moon's reflection in the water. It was kewl. A narrow dock jutted out into the water. Darnell stood on the end of the dock.

Darnell slid his shorts down over his knees. As he leans over, the chain around his neck catches the moonlight. It dangled from his neck. I just looked at him. Darnell looked up at me too. I felt funny. We looked at each other for too long.

"At least you ain't dropped the brew, man."

The lake is wide and deep, like the Great Lakes. I've never seen those lakes or nothin' but I'm guessing this shit up.

Darnell stripped down bare. We did this with the crew at the lake, but now it was just the two of us.

"What are you waitin' for?"

I tore off my boxers and shirt. I kicked off my sneakers. Now, we were both bare-assed naked. I felt a breeze and started to chatter.

Darnell jumped in. I followed. The water felt warm, but when I surfaced the wind made me cold again.

Darnell swam ahead.

"Race you to the raft." The raft floats on oil drums close to the opposite shore.

"Okay."

It was a good swim to there. This time, I knew I was gonna win.

"On your mark, get set, go!"

I leap straight away in the water. I cut across the lake so fast. I'm belly down and panting on the rocking raft when Darnell comes paddling up. He lifts himself onto the raft. He's there, lying beside me. At first we said nothing. I felt my dick stir and so I roll on my belly. My leg hairs snagged while I turned. It hurt like hell. I looked at Darnell's legs. Darnell's dick was as limp as wilted lettuce.

"Damn, I wish I could swim like you."

I reminded him that I was a lifeguard for three years. He then asked me to teach him to save someone from drowning. I explained to him how to tow a victim. Darnell looks at me, bored.

"Nigga please. Show me." He meant in the water.

It was the way he looked at me when he said it. I didn't stand up for fear that he'd see my hard-on. "Swim out there and pretend like you're drowning or something." He turned, shaking his head like he was pissed off, but dove in. I knew if he were far enough away I could dive in and he wouldn't notice my erection.

"Here ok?"

"No, swim out further."

"Here?"

"No, Further and look like you're drowning."

"Mutha Fucka, get in the damn water and act like you're gonna do somethin!"

"You don't look like you're drowning."

When I thought he was looking away. I dove in and swam out past him.

"Brutha, I'm over here."

"This is rule number one. Never approach the victim head-on. He could grab you and drag you down."

"Ok."

I doggy paddled up close behind him. Luckily, my erection had gone down some. I warned him to look ahead. I slipped my left arm over his chest and around his neck. I told him to lie back against me and float. I remember from training, we were told to calm the person, but I didn't say it to Darnell. I stroked the water with my right arm and realized that I would become tired quickly and wished that I hadn't told Darnell to swim out so far. Halfway through, I stopped and said to him I was tired.

"Now let me save you."

Darnell swam around behind me and started to grab me from behind as I did him. I felt my back against his solid chest. I felt his breath on the back of my neck. I allowed myself to float for safety. But instead of doing a safety tow, he floated with me from behind. I felt his whole body touch me. His penis (still soft) against my buttocks.

"Cut it out!" I yelled.

"Why?"

I didn't say anything. My whole body was visible on the surface of the water. His wasn't. There was my erection in the moonlight. I could feel him looking at it. Darnell reaches across and touches my penis, not realizing his change in position made me lose my support. I sink a little. Some water gets into my lungs and I cough. We are now both bobbing face to face, but real close to each other.

However, this time he is looking straight at me. I then feel his dick brushing against my hip. He had an erection too. I reach down to touch it underwater. His dick felt much bigger than mine, which I thought strange, because it didn't look that way when it was soft. It felt enormous in my hand.

Without a word, he swam away from me, back to shore. I was confused but I followed. I don't get it at all. He's the one who started messing with me.

When we were at shore, he started to dress. I dressed too. As we were walking back to the house, Darnell sucker punched me but I didn't fight back. I just pushed him away and kept walking.

We didn't say anything. He then slid his arm across my shoulders. We walked back arm in arm.

The next day, I was real sick. Mom phoned the doctor. Out here, doctors come to your house. He said it was the flu and that I was to rest. I knew that I was sick but I also knew that I had a hangover. I didn't say nothing. I stayed in bed all day. I mostly slept. I couldn't tell if I was dreaming. I could hear, in the distance, my sister and her playmates singing and skipping rope.

I was half-asleep when momma brought some soup, juice and crackers into my room. I felt guilty that I wasn't helping her, and that I broke that bag of flour earlier.

"Momma, you need help downstairs?" I struggled to get up.

"No, no, son. Darnell is here. He knows what to do." She gently pushed me back to bed. Just then, I remembered the lake and the swim. I wondered if I had been dreaming and shit. Momma tucked me in and placed the tray of food on my lap. As she walked from the bed, her foot struck one of the many stones that were on the floor. She looked down at the stones and then at me. Then we were looking at the stones together.

I felt kind of relieved and fell back asleep.

The E-Mail Message

I used to watch Martin "Marty" Lorne play with his pen during our morning sales meetings; how he would hold it with his well-defined fingers. He would roll it back and forth between his thumb and middle finger, sometimes putting it into his mouth. During these moments, I would often say to myself, "What I wouldn't give to be a Bic Pen." Marty was the kind of guy who spoke few words. He always wore nicely pressed shirts that covered his well-defined body. He was quite good-looking with strong Italian features: hairy body, hazel eyes and olive skin. His hair was beginning to recede, which made him more intriguing. I could have watched him all morning.

The morning sales meetings were led by our boss, Sales Manager Gerard Brunel. The meetings were set up to pump enthusiasm in the company's young sales crew. As the meeting broke up, I always tried to find the nerve to think of something to say to Marty other than my usual, "How are sales in your territory?" Our meetings finished around 9:30 a.m. If we didn't have phone calls to make, we were on the road paying visits to our clients. I returned to my cubicle and noticed a flashing internal e-mail message on my computer screen.

It was from Wendy, the company's temp receptionist. She was an old college friend and I helped her get the temp job. She and I held secret crushes on two men in the sales department. Mine was obviously Marty Lorne. Her knight in shining armor was Ken Hollis. Ken was just her type too. I jokingly said to Wendy that Ken was the younger, sexy republican congressman Aaron Schock: blond, clean cut, and conservative. He drove an all-American car—a Ford—and lived in tracked housing in Laguna Nigel, Orange County California, the bastion of republicanism.

I accessed my e-mail from Wendy from my blackberry. Her message read, "Butt Alert!!! Look at how tight Martin's pants are!" Wendy was the sparkle to our dull office. I am sure that my burst of laughter from this message rang out far beyond the walls of my cubicle.

Our company was based in Cerritos, California, and sold integrated plastic parts to local factories in-and-around Southern California. It was your typical L-shaped factory building, with manufacturing on one end of the building and the sales and administration offices on the other. My territory was in the Long Beach area. Our sales crew was like one big happy family. I was one of the newly hired account representatives for the sales department. Ken, Marty, and I were all hired around the same time.

I would try to finish visiting my outside clients early, in order to make it back to the office for lunch. It was summer and everyone sat outside on the makeshift patio. The patio was right beside the warehouse on the parking lot grounds. Southern California was in the middle of a heat wave, a bad smog alert, and the factory workers were shirtless. I could just sit and stare at those well-defined torsos all day. Wendy arrived during her break and whispered, "Jack, you pervert," in my ear as she slid

onto the bench beside me. Wendy
and I would lunch together to
catch up on our latest gossip.
Today Wendy appeared with an
unusually happy glow on her
face. "You are right! Ken just
gave me a change of address form
for the company directory," said
Wendy. "It's Splits-Ville between
him and his wife."

Ken went to my gym. Although
Ken and I never spoke to one
another, Wendy knew that I
almost always had locker room
gossip to report. Ken was quite
handsome but too much of a
family-man type for my liking. I
preferred the more suave type,
like Marty. All I really ever
reported to Wendy, other than his

physical dimensions, was that he hadn't been wearing his wedding ring to the gym. Wendy had dismissed this little bit of information, but I knew a man without his wedding ring was looking for trouble. This meant, "avoid him," in my potential date book, but he was fair game for Wendy.

The following day was another clear and hot day. I was sitting in my usual spot watching the men break from their factory work, when I began to hear a buzzing noise getting louder and louder. Within a moment's notice he appeared in front of me. It was Ken—shirt, tie, helmet and a noisy motorcycle. "Hey! Where's

Wendy?" he shouted over the purring motor. I replied that she should be here shortly. "You like it?" Ken interjected, beaming with pride at his newly acquired Kawasaki Nighthawk. I nodded. "Hop-on, I'll take you for a spin." I thought his offer odd, being that this was the first time Ken and I had ever spoken to each other. I looked around nervously. Having never ridden on a motorcycle, I felt kind of geeky and I didn't want anyone to see me get on it. The bike was far too small for the both of us, and I didn't have a helmet. Ken let the clutch go and the bike jerked into motion. I grabbed the sides of the seat for balance. Ken started to sway the bike left and right. These motions made me abruptly wrap my arms around his waist, because I felt my suit pants slipping on the vinyl seat. Ken rode the bike around the parking lot a few times before returning me to the outside lunching area. Wendy was waiting with a curious look on her face. As I mounted off the bike, my Italian loafers slipped on the asphalt pavement. Ken quickly grabbed my arm, which prevented a complete fall. Wendy, without even asking, hopped on the bike for her turn. Ken gave Wendy the same ride around the parking lot, which seemed to take up our whole lunch break. Wendy and I didn't have much time to talk because I had an appointment with a client right after lunch.

When I returned to the office, I decided to e-mail Wendy a funny message. It read, "Now, if I can only get Marty to ride me like that!"

I sent it to her before turning off my computer to go home. The next day, I felt tension in the meeting room. As I turned for my usual stare at Marty, I noticed he was looking back. He looked rather nervous.

Our Sales Manager Gerard's morning presentation was short. He also passed out a memo. It was from the Human Resources Manager asking that we not play games on other people's internal e-mail. When it was over, Gerard tapped me on the shoulder. "Someone played a silly joke and must have used your computer. You better change your access code," he said as he was leaving. Upon hearing these words, I knew exactly what had happened. The night before, I must have inadvertently sent my e-mail message to everyone instead of Wendy. I felt sick. It wasn't that I was hiding my sexual preference but I wished my closet-opening e-mail message was a little more tactful. For the rest of the day, I was mostly in a daze of guilt. How could I have been so stupid?!

I was only too happy to have finished the day, and to work off some of this tension at the gym. The gym was crowded that night. The rock music and noisy Stairmaster machines seemed to blur together, giving me a migraine headache. My workout was short and painful. As I left the gym and walked to my car, I felt that I forgot something. I thought only of Marty and how he looked back at me during the morning sales meeting. "Could he know how I feel about him?" I wondered.

My headache was killing me. I searched my pockets for car keys only to realize that I had completely forgotten to change out of my gym clothes. My gym bag, keys, and clothes were still in my locker. "Jack, you shithead!" I thought to myself. As I turned towards the gym, Ken appeared from nowhere on his motorcycle. "I think you forgot something," he said while looking at me in my sweaty gym clothes. "Need a lift?" His sarcasm irritated me, but I hopped on his bike out of sheer laziness. Ken released the clutch and the bike rolled to a steady speed towards the gym. I was expecting Ken to ease up on the throttle as we approached the gym building. He didn't. Instead, we sped out past the gym onto the street. The bike kept going faster and faster. I gave my arms a tug around Ken's waist indicating my confusion. The engine roared louder, only breaking its monotonous sound when Ken switched gears. My sweat froze to my body from the oncoming wind. I held Ken tighter and hid behind his body and helmet. "What the fuck are you doing?" I shouted, only to have my voice muffled by the engine. The bike must have been approaching a speed beyond 80 mph because the wind was too strong to maneuver or turn the bike in any direction. I felt that I was in danger, and that this person in front of me was really a stranger. My mind flashed pictures of Pat Buchanan, Rick Santorum, Neo-Nazis, and my e-mail message that Marty and everyone in the office saw. Ken never turned his head once as he maneuvered the bike down side streets, ignoring stop signs. He seemed to be a stranger in a full-faced helmet—almost alien-like. As fast as the ride had started, it was finished. We seemed to have gone full circle, and we were at the front door of the gym. Shaken, I got off the bike. I wobbled to the door. No words were exchanged—or none that I could remember. He just drove off. I promptly went into the men's restroom and vomited. As I puked, all the day's tension seemed to go down the drain. My headache was gone. I quickly grabbed my stuff from the locker and went home. I took a long hot shower and crawled into bed.

The next day, I overslept and missed the morning meeting. I called the office. Wendy answered. I told her about the incident with Ken and she didn't know what to say. I asked her to relay a message to Gerard that I had an early morning client meeting. It was obviously a lie. I hung up the phone and lay in bed, pondering what to do next. For some unknown reason, I was afraid to go to work. I don't see myself as a wimp but still I had this fear. As I stumbled into the kitchen to make coffee, I thought to call the police. I dismissed this due to lack of evidence. I showered, shaved and dressed. I downed my coffee and went to visit some clients. As the day progressed, I felt much better about myself. I returned to work at three that afternoon. The sales section of the office was vacant. I threw my sports coat on my chair. I turned on the computer to check my e-mail messages. Wendy had sent me three messages. Another sales associate, Donald, had sent me two. And I had one from Ken. I froze. I moved my mouse and clicked on his message. There was nothing there. No message. I didn't bother to check the other messages. I just turned off the computer.

I felt helpless and began to panic. I needed some air. I grabbed my jacket and ran outside to the patio. There were some factory workers lounging as I passed them. I was going to my car when I saw his bike. It was just parked there. Passive. I approached the bike, as a mouse would a sleeping cat. I looked back towards the building in time to see Ken exit in my direction. He had a nervous sort of grin on his face. I felt the adrenaline rush through my veins as he approached. I tossed my jacket on the ground. I felt my hands nervously clench into fists. When he was within an arm's reach, I hit him. The punch landed between his nose and upper right cheek. I thought I heard the crack of a bone upon impact. It sent him flying onto his back. I stepped back, in amazement of what I had done, tripping over my coat which lay on the floor. I landed on his bike knocking it off the kickstand onto the ground.

"What the hell was that for?" he said, while muzzling his nose. It was bleeding rather badly. I quickly rose to my feet. "I am not going to take any shit from you or any other hate monger!" I shouted. We were attracting the attention from the loitering plant workers. Within minutes, Wendy and some others were running to us. Ken was whisked inside the office. "Boy, are you going to feel stupid," Wendy said as she picked up my coat. Prior to the scuffle, Ken had just come from speaking with Wendy. Knowing that she was my good friend and feeling reassured from my embarrassing e-mail bungle, Ken confessed to her that he liked me. As Wendy explained this to me, I wanted to crawl under a rock and die. Wendy and I ran back to the office but Ken had already been taken to the hospital.

Wendy and I drove to the Emergency Ward at Norwalk Community Hospital. By the time we found him he was laying on the hospital bed with an ice pack on his nose. The skin had blackened below his eye and his nose was quite swollen. His movements seemed lethargic. Apparently, he had sprained his back on the fall. The doctor had given him Percodan, a very powerful narcotic. As Wendy and I approached Ken, I was thinking of every reason for him not to sue me. He looked at us with sluggish, blood-shot eyes. His face was swollen, but for some reason it attracted me. "I assume Wendy told you the news. I take it I offended you," he said with a grin, "Man, you don't know how much nerve it took for me to talk to her about it." Hearing this conversation, Wendy wandered off to the waiting area. Ken tried to prop himself up, but the drugs worked against him. The irony was that he looked so helpless, "Jack, if you hadn't put your arms around my waist that time on the bike this would never have happened." The drugs made him uninhibited. "I told myself that you touching me meant nothing, but I had to find out," he said. I eased him back into a more lateral position and stroked his hand as if to say enough said. Ken slowly fell asleep. As he slept, I took a good look at Ken and thought to myself about the hell that must be his life right now: leaving his wife, finding himself alone, and being gay. He wasn't discharged until 11:00 p.m. under strict orders for bed rest. Wendy and I took him to my place. We laid him in my bed. I held him all night long. The next day, I watched him sleep while I drank my morning coffee. This stranger who I thought to be an enemy might turn out to be a good friend, and maybe more. He rolled over and opened his eyes. The blackish rings around them made him look funny. I was the first thing he saw. Ken smiled and drifted off to sleep again. Leaving him to recuperate, I went to work. I got to my desk, tossed my jacket into the chair and turned on my computer. There were two flashing e-mail messages, one from Ken and the other from Marty. Ken must have left another message after speaking to Wendy about me. It didn't take me long to decide who to choose.

The message said, "About that ride..."

The Measure of Love

"God!" I say to myself, "I'm doing it again." We have only been dating two months and my mind is already analyzing everything. It's 11:52 a.m. and he's sound asleep right next to me. It's like pulling teeth to get him to even spend the night; it's hard to get any man to spend the night.

So here I am, wide-awake. Thinking. It's always so hard to know who loves you, if you love them back, if they love you enough, if you love them too much, or if the percentages add up or equal out on both sides.

I can't say that any of my dating scenarios have lasted more than three months.

I hear the alarm. I must have eventually drifted off, because it's now morning and the sound is so shocking that it jolts me out of bed. Mike, however, just casually rolls over. The alarm was for him. He has to get ready for work. I am now sitting up in bed and prodding him to wake up. He rolls towards me, curls his arms around my leg and begs for some mercy sleep.

His body has that sweaty morning warmth to it. There is a faintly foul smell of dried drool from him, but I am still glad he is embracing me (or at least my leg). I shake him awake. I feel a sense of duty overruling compassion in my head. I feel I would do a better job of getting to work on-time than snuggling with him. Mike eventually stumbles out of bed and works his way to my bathroom. I hear him as he lifts the toilet seat and makes morning grunts and groans. I hear him urinate. I hear more stumbling noises and eventually the shower makes its familiar rumbling noises.

Again, I lay here. Thinking. I am self-employed and I make my own hours. So I have a lot of idle time. I will go see my friend Harris. Whenever I first see Harris he is cranky, difficult, and bitchy, but he's my own personal project, my own volunteer project of compassion. He is a 67-year-old gay man and I cannot remember how we met. Harris is old and lonely and after being assured he would not take my compassion as some sexual advance, I adopted him. If I hadn't, he would have wasted away with a cigarette and a beer in some dive bar. He's from a generation that believed bar life was where it was at for gay men. In some sense, being gay and at a bar was a way to be hidden or protected from society.

This was our eleventh outing. At first Harris thought I would lose interest and he played along. However, I think we both began to like these "get-togethers." They seem to make our worlds one. We are off to an arboretum today, a sanctuary for trees. Harris is not a nature admirer at all, other than the occasional flowers he'll stop and admire. He sees no reason for such an outing. However, once outside the confines of his smoke-filled old apartment, he eventually brightens up.

Harris is no saint. I keep a blind eye to his occasional rent boys that I often have to scurry off when I fetch him for our outings. Our outings were difficult at first because we had trouble relating to each other, but we never gave up. There was something important to each of us in continuing to make this work. It was like two diverging men from the great gay divide were finding common ground. His generation saw coming out as the biggest single event in a gay man's life, and had to experience the loss of cherished friends due to AIDS; my generation faced Xbox, MySpace, and gay marriage as its characterizing themes.

"You didn't sleep well," Harris says as we are walking down Gerrard Street making our way to the park.

"I'm dating someone and it's so fucking hard," I say. I repeat what I said last night about who loves more.

"Ah," he adds, "the measure of love." I have never heard Harris speak about love. He would often tell me of his youth and sexual escapades. Harris sensed my heavy heart.

"Have you ever been in love Harris?" I ask.

"Not really, I guess I was too selfish," he replies. Harris lights a cigarette. I don't smoke. I hate smoking. I move to his other side to be away from the smoke that trails from his smoking. "I had my opportunities, but only realized when it was too late." Harris is familiar with my efforts to find true love. He feels it's a vain attempt, but keeps this thought a secret. "What is love to you?" I asked him. He was silent for the duration of the walk. He was reminiscing and a nostalgic sadness fell upon him.

He stopped and looked at me and said, "I know you want to go to the park but I could really use a beer." I wasn't happy with the request, but acquiesced. We pulled into some unfamiliar restaurant and sat at the bar. You know the type, a seating area for meals and a bar area with stools. I don't like stools. They hurt my back so I asked if we could sit at a table on the restaurant side. It was 10:00 in the morning and I couldn't think about drinking. The bar had old pine wood and beaten-up chairs. The stale smell of the bar was so powerful that it permeated through the entire place. As we sat, a heavyset girl walked up to us with menus, but Harris just brushed them aside as she handed them over. He ordered a Budweiser and I just asked for water. Bemused by her lack of a meal tip, she walked off soon to return with a tall glass of golden beer and my ice water. We were the only ones in the bar. Harris tossed a few dollars on her tray and she strolled off.

"Hey," he gestured after a long silence, "are you ok?"

"Funny," I replied, "I was just about to ask you the same thing."

"Oh my dear boy, of course I'm ok. I was just taking a trip down memory lane. It's not a good thing to do at my age. You see how much time as passed you by."

Harris takes a swipe of his beer. He wipes his beer mustache away. "And you?" he asks.

I don't know why, but I suddenly felt the urge to pour out my feelings on life and love. I don't know how it would work for any gay man and I. "Gay men are just not meant for relationships," I concluded.

Harris has given up on love long ago. I expected he'd say something along those lines, but instead I saw compassion from him. Compassion I had never seen before.

"Don't dismiss all of them Rob," he said, "you only need one good one; just one. You asked me about love earlier." He takes another sip of his beer. "I know love, or I know the secret to love, anyway. Ninety percent of people, not just gay men, get love wrong. Love is simple. Love is what you are willing to do for someone else, end of story. It is a selfless act for selfless people. Now, should you meet someone who is willing to be as selfless for you as you are for them, then it is mutual love and it's a bonus. So don't measure, just give of yourself and don't expect anything in return and be happy for it."

I ponder his wisdom. I wouldn't have imagined him ever saying such things.

I began to respond, "you know you could have…," but he interrupted me.

"Remember, I'm selfish, and I'm fine without love. Don't worry about me. However, I see you rolling with the heartbreaks and getting back on that path again. You get a lot of points for trying kid. You are a good egg."

I blush at the compliment and try to hide my giggle over the last statement, particularly at the word "egg."

"From what I have seen, strong relationships are a competition of generosity, my boy." With those final words he finished his last drop of beer and got up to go. "Now, how about that walk" he says.

I get up feeling so much better. I go to hug Harris. As I embrace him warmly, he lightly hugs back, wearing an expression that almost says, "It's too late for me, save yourself."

However, I was saving Harris. I made a promise that Harris will always have me as friend and family.

We continued on our path, each happy for the other.

Oh Shit!

_____

It's not often that a gay man has the opportunity to reject the advances of a straight man, but I did. It wasn't for the reasons that many would have thought, either. Tom is straight, but he's just curious. "You're a fuckin' idiot," was Tom's reply to my rejection. He wasn't angry. He's not even curious about gay sex. He's just curious about me. He was curious about me being Afro-American, American, a guy, and yet different from him. I just don't know exactly what it was, but there was chemistry between us.

Tom had a potty mouth on him. My mother is an English professor. I have never sworn in my life.

"You got to be fuckin' kiddin' me, you never swore?" he once asked during one of our many conversations. It is true. When the rare occasion came for me to swear, I would just do it using an ancient Greek or Latin word. To me, no one knew what I was saying and I was smugly comfortable knowing it.

Tom and I met at the restaurant where we both worked. He actually trained me when I first got there. His gaydar did not pick up on me. He is used to guys and girls hitting on him. I had just arrived in town and was $33,000 in debt, with a bank account that had $28.00 in it. So admiring Tom's sexiness was the least of my interests.

He liked my humour. When I made mention of something concerning Queer as Folk, he slapped his hand on the table and said, "Fuck you James, I knew you were gay." I brushed off the comment and we continued on with the conversation we were having.

One day Tom and I had the same shift, and I got to see him kiss his girlfriend Lisa. She was pretty. I thought her face was cute but the nose ring didn't really enhance her features. She was considerably shorter than he. I remember thinking that her calves were too big for her diminutive stature.

Tom and I worked at a busy Italian dining restaurant. I've never been a fan of Italian restaurants. After all, why pay $40.00 for a meal that you can put together at home for $5.00. Besides, I also think pasta prematurely ages your skin. Actually, I think this about all carbohydrates in general. Since I could stand to lose a few pounds, I was a little weight conscious.

For me, the act of getting dressed is an art of illusion. I wear dark colors and buy underwear with huge waist bands that I place to conceal my love handles. This entails me hoisting the waist band above my hips, and thus killing the circulation to my balls.

Tom and I developed a nice friendship. He's very approachable and has an optimistic view of everything. About an hour into our shift one night, Tom leans in and says, "You ever notice that the gay servers touch when they pass each other, but the straight guys never do?" I told him that I never gave it any thought.

The night that I rejected him, he was drunk. We had had an after work get-together. There are a string of bars in this district and our staff often goes out and gets plastered after work. Tom and Lisa live in the suburbs. I live within walking distance from the restaurant and it was almost 4 a.m. by the time we were stumbling back to my place. It was just Tom and myself. Tom kept saying what a "fucking awesome guy" I was all night at the bar. Everyone just laughed at his repetitiveness.

"You're such a fucking awesome guy," he slurred as drool fell from him mouth. As I was struggling to open the door, Tom leaned in and kissed me. "We'll have none of that," I said. He laughed. He tried it again, but I pushed him away.

I have to admit the thought about having something deeper with Tom was intriguing, but I didn't want to think about it at that moment.

"Look, I'm flattered," I say in the most sober manner that I can muster. "I don't deal with these 'down low' situations too well." He says ok and repeats again how, "Fucking awesome," he thinks I am.

The next morning, as we are nursing our headaches and he was trying to leave, Tom apologized for the previous night. I told him not to worry, that we are friends. He was very comfortable in his apology. Our friendship is rather open and trusting, which is why he felt at ease about the night before.

We actually hung out quite often. Tom's really a "techy" type, which can bore the daylights out of me sometimes. He's creating his own gaming software, and it involves some unique idea he feels will set him above the rest. The good thing about Tom is that when we are together, he can tell when he's getting too "techy" on me and changes the subject. Lisa, his girlfriend, works in a daycare. They fit well together, and we have had many nights of sheer fun and laughter between the three of us. "You're fuckin awesome," he would always say.

A few months later, it was my night off and I was really intent on a night of ice cream, pretzels (yes, I know, carbs), beer and whatever was playing on American Movie Classics. I love old movies, but found the first movie a real bore, and couldn't even tell you who the main actors were. I wasn't familiar with any of them. My mind drifted away from the programming and into my personal thoughts. I was on my fourth beer when the phone rang. It was Tom. "Hey, get your ass over here, Lisa and the gang from the restaurant are at the B Bar, come join us."

I told Tom that I was in my sweats and T-shirt already, and would need to get dressed. His pleading softened me a bit and I agreed to meet them. "Us" consisted of Tom, Lisa, Billy and Darnell. Billy is straight and Darnell is gay. The B Bar was crowded, noisy, and very straight. It's not our typical bar, but that one closed early last month for renovations. The B Bar was poorly designed, with the bar in the back, down a narrow corridor. The building is L-shaped, which doesn't allow for people to mingle freely.

I honestly never really thought about Tom in a physical manner until that night. I was slightly buzzed and in a reflective mood. He really is a handsome guy, the kind who doesn't know how handsome he is. He's just happy in his own skin. He never says a bad word about anyone. You'd think he was Mormon, except for the fact he has tattoos everywhere, drinks, and swears all the time.

Lisa spots me and motions me over to the bar. "Tom's not drinking," she says, "He's the designated driver." She orders herself a martini and two beers, which I presume are for Billy and Darnell. "What will you have?"

Lisa yells into my ear to make up for the loudness around us. I tell her that I'll buy, but she refuses. She then tells me how Tom told her about my budget and how I'm trying not to spend too much money. I give in and order a scotch and soda. "You know Tom really likes you," Lisa again yells into my ear. "I like him too," I reply. "You're lucky."

Our drinks arrive and Lisa pays. We work our way from the back to the front of the long narrow passageway, to where Tom and the rest of the gang are. I see Tom has bottled water. I have never seen Tom at a bar without a beer or some type of alcoholic drink in his hand. Tom is seated against the wall farthest from Lisa and me. He was wedged in by Billy, who is also a big gamer type. You can tell they were talking about some new game for Xbox as we arrived. Darnell was scoping the bar looking for gay men. He seemed to always act like he's doing us a favor when he comes out with us. However, he is really happy to hang out with us because it gives him a break from his bitchy, queenly friends.

Tom waves a jovial hello to me without breaking the conversation with Billy. Lisa passes out the drinks, but just then Tom proposes a toast. "To Fuckin' kewl James, for getting out of his house clothes and joining us." We all clicked bottles, except for Tom's water bottle, which made no sound.

B Bar is full of Eurotrash, and not even the classy types. They are mainly eastern Europeans on summer work visas, serving the various hotels and restaurants in this tourist trap of a city we live in.

Darnell is making fun of them, and he's really on. We are laughing at the funny descriptions that he gives each person that parades past us. "Look at Svetlana over there; she's doing 1970s disco in her gold lamé," Darnell whispers. We all laugh.

Just then a server glides into the crowd. Tom stops her and asks, "Could you get us a round of tequila, lime and salt please?" She nods in acknowledgement, but doesn't ask how many. She hurries off and is back with five shot glasses of tequila, lime wedges and salt. Tom rises and digs into his pocket and pulls out a wad of crumpled twenties to pay her. "Oh, James man, take my shot because I can't drink." I flash him a look but happily take the shot anyway.

We salt the tops of our hands, take our shots, lick the salt, and suck on the limes. We all slam our glasses down and howl. The Eurotrash around us turn in our direction with disapproving looks. We all laugh. The server is within shouting distance and Billy orders another round. She returns again with five shot glasses of tequila. "I can't," and Tom was pawning off the fifth glass to me. I pass it to Billy who passes it to Lisa.

"No, let Lisa take it," Billy shouts. Again, we salt the tops of our hands, take our shots, lick the salt, and suck on the limes. Again, we all slam our glasses down and howl. The Eurotrash around us turn to us again with disapproving looks, and this time some of them walk away. We are all laughing uncontrollably.

The server was smart or Tom was tipping well, because she made sure she wasn't far from us, and Tom ordered again. I told the server to only bring four shots this time. However, she returned with five shot glasses claiming that she forgot. "This one's on me," she said. Tom again reaches and slides the glass to me. I in turn slide it to Darnell, who gives it back to me.

"Your precious Tom wants you to have it," he says suspiciously. I correct him saying that Tom is Lisa's special guy, not mine. I am beginning to notice that I'm slurring my words.

"Fuck you asshole, I'm not precious to you James?" Tom yells from afar. This makes Billy, Lisa, and I laugh. We are definitely drunk by now. Darnell sees someone and leaves us to go greet them.

I was feeling dizzy, and told them that I should go home. Lisa pouts and Billy simply ignores my announcement. Tom scoots Billy so that he can come and give me a hug goodbye, but instead he says that he'll walk me home.

I protest, telling him that I live 4 blocks from here and that nothing will happen. Lisa sort of interjects and reminds me that Tom is the designate, and that we must all listen to him because he's sober. Tom hasn't walked me home alone since that night he made a pass at me. I figured it was an awkward moment never to be repeated, because we cherished our friendship so much.

As he was leaving, he gives Lisa his remaining cash and a credit card. "I'll be back, but enjoy the moment while I'm gone," he says. I'm stumbling as we walk through the crowd. I was drunker than I had realized. At one point, Tom had to steady me. He was so gentile with me and yet so strong.

As we were walking to my place, we were laughing about the stares we got from the Euro trash. As

I'm fumbling with my keys, Tom is leaning against the side wall of the apartment entrance way.

"You know James, this time will be different." "What will be different?" I ask, not really paying attention as I work the key into the keyhole.

"Us," Tom says sternly. I had successfully opened the door and we were now walking in the hallway of my complex. While I'm stumbling Tom is walking. I was so drunk that I forgot what he was talking about.

My keys are in my hand and I'm about to fumble again with another key hole when Tom takes them from me and opens the door with sober-man precision.

I walk past him into my living room. I was in such a hurry earlier that I left all the lights on, and the television was still playing classic movies. The ice cream had all melted. I offered Tom a beer, forgetting that he was not drinking. I turn off the television, and then there is this awkward silence.

I turn to Tom, who is staring at me. It was then that I realized that this entire evening was planned. I know him well enough to see through him, and he knew it. I smiled coyly thinking he was going to make fun of me, but he didn't smile back. Instead, he reached into his pocket, retrieved his cell phone and called Lisa. I heard her answer.

"Lisa, James is a little sick and I think I should stay behind," he lies. "Do you mind taking a cab home? I gave you $80.00 and the visa, which should be enough for a few more drinks." She offers to come over but Tom refuses.

Like a man being pulled over by the cops, I try to sober myself to get control of the situation.

"James, I need to tell you something," Tom starts. I interject for safety reasons, "Tom, you're not gay." We both laugh. He comes closer to me and I back away. I am casing the surroundings. I think about drunken women and the straight men who rape them. I say out loud, "So, this is how it feels."

"What?" Toms asks inquisitively. I dismiss it as I'm angling to dart into the kitchen. I can feel my heart beating. I'm thinking to myself that this isn't really happening. I'm also thinking this is some other gay guy's fantasy, not mine. I chuckle to myself.

"Dude, don't be a dick, you know how great I think you are."

I am trying to talk Tom out of this, but I can tell this has been on

his mind for quite some time. I
am feeling stupid. I am feeling
foolish and trying to think of the
words that will make this not
happen.

However, I am drunk, and do
what drunks do most, make dumb
decisions.
I jolt right towards the kitchen,
climbing over the couch, but I
miss my step and go crashing to
the floor bringing an end table
and a lamp down with me.

Tom curses and goes to aid me.
"Shit, are you OK?" he asks in a
concerned manner. I feel my head
is spinning and my nose is
bleeding. Tom rushes into the
kitchen and grabs the paper

towels. We pinch the towel over my nose to stop the bleeding. I remain on the floor, while Tom sits in the lotus position and pulls a pillow from the couch. He places the pillow on his lap and I lay inclined there to stop the bleeding.

I try to sound intelligent and I tell him that sex ruins everything. He apologizes and we sit in silence. He reaches for my hand and holds it. In despair, he says, "Man, I really like you. I don't know, or maybe it could be love. Fuck, I wish in some way I could express it so that you'd understand."

"I like you too Tom, which is why I am telling you that we shouldn't do this."

I know he loves Lisa. They have been together for three years. I think I should get the Mother Theresa award for such selflessness.

I tell Tom that I'm beat and we should sleep. I tell him that he can sleep on the couch, and he does after helping me into my bed. He turns out the lights and I quickly drift into a deep sleep.

At some point during the night, Tom climbs into bed with me and we spoon as we sleep. Our clothes are still on. It is daylight when I first realize all of this. I get up to pee and realize I have a wicked headache.

I flush the toilet and I crawl back into bed with Tom. I'm still tired. We cuddle.

"Thanks," he says.

"For what?" I ask.

"For coming back to bed with me." I really didn't think about the couch as an option, but I did not dare to say that. Tom's emotions are raw right now. He's dealing with a lot, I figure. I ask him if he planned this and he admitted that he did.

He asked me to accept this, and not to be angry.

"I'm not angry. I'm not sad either," I mumble while trying to sleep.

"Tell you what Tom," I say, "I'll make you a promise."

"What is the promise?" he says.

"When you wake up tomorrow with a clear head, and if you still feel that you have these feelings for me, I'll give an honest try to see if this can work."

"Deal," he replies. He smiles. His eyes are closed while smiling.

Happy that I settled the matter, instead of running away from it, I begin to drift off to sleep again until I realize.

"Oh shit!" I shout out loud as I open my eyes. I forgot that Tom was sober.

I could see in the morning light Tom eyes were closed but his smile was getting wider.

"Tom, you motherfucker!"

The Abyss

Vast, deep blue waters on a TV screen caught my eye as I entered the teahouse, distracting my attention for a moment. It took a few seconds before I noticed that he was waving at me from a corner booth.

The problem was that he looked exactly like me; we could almost pass for brothers. He was visibly shaken by this, and I was shocked as well. My ex had replaced me with someone who looked just like me but who was not me at all. I guessed that he must be constantly compared to me, which would be unnerving. It was also sad, since he was younger and well dressed. I liked his look, though; he appeared narcissistic, but the clothes he had on really complimented him. I thought that I should wear clothes like that. "You're older than I expected," he said dryly. I didn't know if he was saying this as a put down or just an acknowledgment. I could smell the scent of cigarettes on his breath. I don't smoke. I'm sure that Doug did not approve of his smoking.

This person had found me. I hadn't known he existed until he called me about meeting. He seemed a little desperate; he needed peace in his relationship. I knew Doug, and knew also that he didn't know how to make his boyfriends feel good, or secure when they were with him.

Still, I felt that it was not my place to warn him about Doug; perhaps Doug had changed. My goal was to feel nothing for Doug, not even hate. It is truly when you feel nothing that you forget the person. I tried to explain that I was there for him, not for Doug. "My time with Doug was nice, but it ended in disaster," I said. "He dumped me, for which I'll never forgive him."

I felt that it wasn't what he wanted to hear. He didn't want to sympathize with me. He wanted Doug to be the victim. He wanted to think that I was just some selfish, self-loathing fag looking to do battle with him. I wasn't.

I tried a different approach. "I don't know what I can do to make you feel better. I guess you should know that it would never have worked between Doug and me. I was too old. I was like a parent he didn't want or need."

This backfired. His face flushed and he raised his voice in anger, only to lower it after it drew attention from the other patrons of the teahouse.

"He thinks that you were his soul mate," this stranger retorted. "He says this often when he's drunk. He talks about you a lot."

We were silent for a minute. He stared into his cup. Twirled it a bit and watched the liquid spin inside.

We've all been there: a guy comparing you to his ex. It's unnerving. I tried to reassure him. "Doug is only looking at the good parts. Most of our time together was composed of unhappy moments, for the both of us," I replied.

He remained silent and continued to stare into his teacup. I looked around to occupy the silence that grew between us.

At one table, a mother was talking with her girlfriend while her daughter stood beside them, rocking from one foot to another. The girl was obviously bored, but they seemed to have a strong bond; the mother stroked her daughter's hair as she talked.

At another table, a young man in a business suit talked on his cell phone. He seemed disconnected from the other patrons in the teahouse, as he ignored what he had ordered, and continued to be engrossed by some business deal on the phone.

In the back of the shop was the large flat screen television that had caught my attention earlier. Two divers were exploring the ocean floor. The camera caught amazing views of colourful fish swimming by. The face of the diver holding the camera was never shown; all you saw was his occasional hand wave ahead. The other diver swam far ahead of the cameraman. His figure disappeared from view in the dark water, and you saw only the light from his diving mask.

My eyes returned to the stranger before me. I saw no easy resolution to this conversation. If I were blunt and direct, I would have told him to leave Doug. Doug's issues couldn't be fixed by anyone but himself. The person in front of me had simply been used to satisfy some idea of Doug's that had never really existed. I thought of the song "Prisoner of Love" by James Brown, and how love in these circumstances really hurts. I sighed. "I should go," I said. "I'm sorry about what you're going through."

He appeared dismayed, wanting me to stay longer. He offered to buy me a drink but I declined. His exhausted and deflated look told me that I had been his only hope. As I exited the teahouse, I felt his eyes watch me leave. Alone, he was left to dwell in that lonely abyss where most find themselves at some point. An abyss where love no longer seems to exist, and the only way out is a long journey, up through the dark cold waters, hoping that there will be daylight when you reach the surface.

The Understanding

If you were to ask him if he was heterosexual, he would say yes. He was a student and claimed to be 27 years old. He answered my Craigslist post which read "Looking for Straight Curious." When he appeared at my door, he had the right amount of discomfort and stature for me to be convinced that he hadn't done this often.

I had offered him beer and 420. He took both in heavy doses. As he got comfortable, he started to tell me more about himself. "You know I'm really 31," he said. I pretended to be shocked and said in protest, "Just for that, you won't know my age." The truth was that I lied about my age in the Craigslist ad that he answered. He really wanted to know but he dropped it. He was studying something at BCIT. He looked like a student. He told me that he had a girlfriend for the last 4 years, and that they just broke up, or were in the process. She is Asian. I always felt that non-Asian guys who dated Asian women seemed more likely to be bisexual than most.

In the course of our conversation, I moved my hand to touch him, which gave him the freedom to do the same. However, he reached directly for my crotch. He had an erection that was visible through

his jeans. I kept on speaking as
he massaged my crotch.
He was handsome, but guarded. I
could tell that he was in uncharted
territory. "You know I've only
been with three guys," he told me.
I lied and hinted that I was
bisexual, this put him at ease. I
figured if I told him the truth, that
I was gay, it would have made
him more uncomfortable. This
reality angered me.
It was the picture on my wall that
threw him. It was an oil painting
and had a man and woman nude.
The picture was my alibi. I was
determined to remain a mystery
for him. He didn't know exactly if
I was truly bisexual or really gay.
He didn't know my age. I knew
that in casual hook-ups, part of

the attraction is the mystery and the illusion. He knew I liked sports, and challenged me to a basketball game, but that was not one of the sports in which I excelled. Had he said tennis or even darts, I would have taken him on the challenge. Physically, he was noticeably thinner than me. He liked that, but also had to reassure me that he wasn't a wimp. He flexed his arm muscle to show his biceps. "You know, I win a lot of arm wrestling matches," he said with pride. He was of Scottish descent and had rugged, handsome looks. Here is where I envied him. He was passing as a solid heterosexual male but clearly he is bisexual. He had all the qualities of a straight guy that I myself could pull off, but I don't. To me, that sort of life is a sad existence. He and I had sex. Great sex. I showed him new things. He thanked me and I saw desire in his eyes. I was content when I saw this emotion, because I wanted to share that I really liked him, and would perhaps date him, but I knew the rules of the game. The rules told me not to show any desire in return. He was the first to break the rules, as he hinted that he wanted to see me again, and I avoided commitment. However, the reality was that I really wanted to see him again. However, I knew this would make me the loser. He was a player on both sides of the fence, showing an inability to be monogamous. I would want all or nothing, but he didn't know that. He left a little disappointed that it didn't develop into something to his liking, but that is the one thing women had taught me about the opposite sex. You must treat straight boys with the desire to want more. Afterwards, I checked his Facebook profile from time to time. It shows vibrant pictures of him, his girlfriend, their trips and their lives. However, I looked into his eyes and saw emptiness. I often asked myself if I was fooling myself or if he was fooling himself. People can convince themselves that they are happy in any situation. With him, I wasn't so easily fooled.

Earl's Child

When the county school board
ordered black children to be
educated, all the white teachers
flat out refused. They refused, not
because we were black, but
because the pay was too low. In
those days the county simply did
not employ black teachers.
It was about two months into the
school year, and Earl Perkins took
the position to teach 11 black
children in a one-room
schoolhouse built just for us. Earl
Perkins was his real name, but
everyone in town called him
Mearl, and they would snicker
when they said it, like it was

some kind of private joke. I heard that Mearl got his nickname because people would call him, "Miz Earl." I suppose as time wore on, his nickname just naturally became Mearl.

Earl Perkins had odd ways. He was a very tall, thin, white man with a long, narrow nose. He was what I guess you would call effeminate. Momma preferred the word soft, probably because she didn't know what effeminate really meant. Momma couldn't read or write. Never did have the chance to learn how. But I did not care. It was because of the late, great Earl that I would later go on to graduate from Villanova University with honors.

Earl lived on the outskirts between the towns of Kingston and Hurley in the great State of New York. He lived on a small self-sufficient farm with a man called Midges. No one knew his real name or even his last name, because no one cared. It was common knowledge that they were a couple. Two men. No women. A farm. I am sure it was frowned upon, but I never heard anyone mention them or their relationship. "Good Morning, Ms. Winters," Earl would say to the clerk at the only general store in town. "My Midges said he wants steak tonight, can you imagine?" Earl always referred to Midges as, "My Midges." Earl didn't care what people thought. Earl had all he needed, or at least all he thought he needed.

Earl was one of the few folk in this area that had a university degree that wasn't working. He had a degree in teaching from the newly-established New York State University, which would later be called State University of New York (SUNY). Every day Earl would go to the school board looking for work and every day they would tell him that there were no jobs available. Even when he had heard that teachers from out of town had arrived to fill posts that he knew he had applied for, he was undaunted in believing that the system would somehow respect him.

Earl eventually did get a job. A teacher to 11 black school children in the only schoolhouse that would have us. I was one of five children in my family, but the only one that my parents could spare to educate. My family used to collect the garbage from the neighboring white towns and deliver it to the county dump. This was how we made our living, you see, with two dilapidated trucks that were rusty and generated more smoke than a forest fire, I don't mind saying. However, on the hill, we were considered well off because we had vehicles, even if they were old.

Every day, Earl went up that hill. He wasn't fearful of us like the other white folk. He wasn't fearful of our community either. He was stern, but respectful. Most black parents didn't put much creed in schooling and therefore only sent one or two of their children. The remaining children had to work. All the families on the hill were poor financially, but rich in spirit, our church reverend would say. So Earl was my first teacher, and the best one I had ever had.

I remember he wore the oddest outfits. He had a tight dark jacket that didn't fit his long arms very well. He wore a white shirt and a yellow bow tie that was too big. His shoes were work boots with patches on the soles.

On his first day of school, he walked into the classroom and wrote his name in chalk on the school board. MR. PERKINS (just like that). I remember only seeing a chalk board once when I was sent to help the Anderson family clean the white schools in town while Mrs. Anderson got her health back, after some surgery. She actually died shortly afterward, and others were found to help clean the school.

Earl Perkins neatly wrote in capital letters on the chalk board, and promptly sat upon his elevated seat at his elevated desk. He looked us over and then he had each of the 11 children introduce themselves by name. We did. He then asked us to introduce ourselves to the class, and tell everyone what we wanted to be when we grew up. We thought it was stupid because we all knew each other. When it was my turn, I raised my hand.

"Mr. Perkins," I said.

"What is it dear?" he asked.

"I don't think I want to do this because we ain't ever getting off this mountain," I replied.

He asked for my name again and he looked at me and then asked if I could get off this mountain what would I want to be?

"My name is Eloise Le May and I want to become a banker," I said.

Everyone laughed.

"How did you come to this conclusion?" he said.

I assumed that meant why, because I didn't know what conclusion meant. I said, "no one here has money, and my Momma said the banker has all the money." The class laughed again. Mr. Perkins moved away from his seat and walked over to me. I started to shake because I thought he was gonna get a switch and beat me. However, he kindly leaned over and said to me: "Ms. Eloise Le May, you can come off this mountain, go to university, and become a banker if that is what you wish."
I didn't believe him. But he didn't make me stand up in front of the room either, which made me feel special.

One day I had passed a math test he had given us with 100 percent. He placed it on the class board with a thumbtack to hold it up. In big red letters, he marked "100%" and then the word "SMART" and circled it.

"See Ms. Eloise Le May, you got the workings of a banker in you." He called me smart, which I will never, ever forget.

After that I didn't want to let Mr. Perkins down. It was the first time that I felt anyone ever believed in me. I made sure that I would not let Mr. Perkins down. I studied and passed every test he gave me with flying colors. Truth be told, I had a little crush on Mr. Perkins. I was naïve to the fact that he was not partial to women, but as a child you don't know of such things. I didn't come to these discoveries until much later.

He was our teacher for three years. I saw him walk the 7 miles from his and Midge's farm up the hill to our one-room school house. On snowy days, rainy days and just plain cold days, we knew for sure Mr. Perkins would be at our school. Soon the black folk grew to trust him. When meals were made, extra was brought to him. He was equally kind. When Mrs. Trusset, the widower, came down with whooping cough, Mr. Perkins knitted her a scarf and a shawl. He knitted right there in front of us while teaching. He never missed a beat, in either his knitting or his lesson plan. I was thoroughly amazed by him.

One day, Carol Chambers' daughter came back from being ill. To everyone's surprise, she had a newborn with her. It was a baby boy, and she named him Staton. She never told anyone who the father was. Well, not long after she got sick, and made the baby and her own Momma sick. They all died, except for the baby. It was Mr. Perkins who stepped in and took the baby, before the white townsfolk found out. Had the white townsfolk known, the baby would have been put into the orphanage. Nobody knew that the baby carried whatever sickness Carol Chambers and her daughter died from. Mr. Perkins knew, and he didn't care. He would carry little Staton in a basket from school the entire 7 miles home, and back again the very next day. He would teach us while feeding the baby. He was truly a person who believed he could do anything. The black women of our community helped out too. They gave Mr. Perkins old clothes, extra food or whatever they could spare to help him with raising little Staton. One thing was for certain, Mr. Perkins was happy that he had this black baby. He mothered it like no mother ever could, and that baby loved him. He knitted outfits for little Staton to wear, and would talk baby-talk to him right in front of us. He called him, "My Staton," just like he referred to Midge as, "My Midge."

However, the black folk knew that baby was cursed, and refused to touch it. Soon Mr. Perkins grew ill. It was from that baby. We knew it. Mr. Perkins grew weak, and paler with each passing day. He got so weak that Midge would take him on the carriage to-and-from the school to their home. However, Midge soon got sick too, and could no longer make the trip. Soon the townsfolk started driving him to our school house and some of the few black families that owned horse and carriage would take him home. It broke poor Mr. Perkins' heart when he had to give up both teaching and the baby. The baby went on to an orphanage, and Earl and Midge were diagnosed with acute tuberculosis. They were soon sent to sanitariums, where they died shortly after being separated.

By then, the county school board placed a black teacher to teach us. She was from the South. She was mean, fat and strict. She also taught us scriptures. I missed Mr. Perkins, and vowed to get off this mountain and get an education. The baby that Mr. Perkins and Midge cared for never got ill. He was in the Kingston orphanage for a time. The only black baby there. When he was old enough they brought him back to our school. He was abused him.

Staton had just started school when I was leaving it. By this time, I was graduating and off to university. I was the first person in my family to ever get a university degree.

I worked in the tax collector's office, because no bank in town trusted a black person with their money, let alone a black woman. I eventually found work far away in Brooklyn, New York. I soon married and was raising a family of my own. New York was full of different people and cultures. After 15 years of hard work, I became this bank's first ever black branch manager. My Momma would have been so proud! I was even featured in Jet

Magazine for my accomplishment.

One day, I received a phone call in my office, and it was from a Mr. Staton Perkins, applying for a home mortgage. He was married and buying a house in Jamaica, New York. He had heard that I was from Hurley, where he was from, and wanted to ask for some assistance. He had graduated from university, and was now a young up-and-comer attorney at a firm in New York City. He carried Mr. Perkins' last name and not his mother's. I believe he did this because the people at the orphanage never knew his real last name.

I often wonder how different my life would have been if Mr.

Perkins did not believe in me. If he did not tell me that I was, "100% SMART," and that I could get off that mountain. I met Mr. Staton Perkins and his lovely wife Kelli Marie to sign the mortgage documents. She was seven months pregnant at the time. I don't think he ever knew that he was raised on a farm by two men that loved him like their own. I don't think he knew that he was a carrier of some virus that killed his mother, grandmother, my beloved Mr. Perkins, and Mr. Perkins' beloved Midges. I smiled and congratulated them on their new home. As they left, I told Staton Perkins that if he had a boy that they should name him Earl. I told him that this was a man who

I knew loved him very much, but is no longer with us. I also told him that I would not be here today had it not been for Earl's encouragement. Staton and Kelli Marie thanked me for the advice. I do not know if they had a boy or girl because I never saw them again. I guess I was happy enough to tell Staton how much Earl had loved him, which is all that mattered in the end.

The Wrong Voice Far Away – Egypt

First Published "SBC Magazine," WINTER EDITION 2001

It was a journey that I thought would never end. A journey to the homeland of my mother. It was a hot, endless journey along the Nile from the Egyptian city of Asyut by caravan. The caravan would have several overnight rest stops. The sites were uncomfortable, flea infested, dimly lit and the food was awful. I would lie awake at night wondering why I was there. The journey was to pay respects to my mother's family, as her father, a man I did not know, had died. I was the only one of my 13 brothers and sisters who was able to go. My mother, a housewife, told me that she was of noble stock from a nomad tribe of what is now known as southeastern Sudan and western Ethiopia.

She married an Egyptian, my father, who was a merchant at the time. He's now a statesman, and with such a position comes arrogance. He has adopted Western ways and Western thinking from the British occupiers. It was easier for him to change to the British lifestyle. He was a Christian. He looked down on my mother's culture and forbade her to tell us anything about it. His insolence overshadowed his heart, for he forbade my mother to attend her own father's funeral.

To be honest, I had no interest in going. However, when I last visited my mother, her cries and pleas that her favorite son go overpowered both my reason and disinterest.

I remember telling Mohammad that I was to go and that it would be one month's journey. He said nothing. Three weeks before I was to leave, I told him again, and still he said nothing. He wasn't a man of many words, which annoyed me. He got up from the bed, as he did every evening, and went to the bathroom. He washed himself in preparation for prayer. I remember the dim light blinding me to his figure in the bathroom. It was my bathroom. Quietly, Mohammad washed his face, hands, and feet and came into the bedroom. I was angry at him. I paid the rent. Muslims always brought their own sujada—special prayer rugs. It always disturbed me, his praying like this in my bedroom. As he kneeled facing the same direction – just as he did every night from my room for the last 6 months he'd been with me – I would prop myself up on one arm and watch him from the bed. I studied his beauty. His brown skin that had a sort of reddish hue. Lips so big and black you'd swear they were painted. The contrast was striking on him. His hair in thick black curls. Like me, he was a mix of African colours, cultures, and influences. I want to say that he also looked like me but that would be a lie.

When he was done praying, he went back to the bathroom and washed himself again. He returned to bed. We had sex. As we were resting, Mohammad reached underneath the bed and presented me with a brown scroll; on it were 25 poems written by Tarafah ibn al-'Abd. It was tied with a single red ribbon, with a flower lodged in the knot of the bow. Mohammad read me poem

#6 and poem #10 as I lay there in amazement. It was poem #10 that made me smile. It made us laugh together. The poem was beautiful in some ways, even though it made light fun of desert people. This scroll was a gift. He had never given me anything before - nothing to acknowledge my existence as anything other than a friend. He said that it was for my journey, but I knew it meant more. I was astonished at my realization that for the last six months Mohammad and I had made love, not just sex. These last 6 months, Mohammad viewed this as his home and me as his partner. I knew that, most of all, this gift meant he would miss me.

I remembered that last night with
Mohammad well as I lay in my
flea-infested tent wanting the
journey to end. I was at my third
campsite. That night seemed so
long ago. Mohammad's voice
was soft and sweet as he read me
the poems in Arabic. There were
25 poems written side by side on
the leather scroll. It must have
cost him what little he had. I fell
asleep each night with the scrolls
in my arms.

Mohammad's voice was but a
distant memory as the hot sun
beat upon the scarf-covered heads
of passengers in an overcrowded
cart that followed the dirt road
which ran along the Nile. Farm
animals trailed alongside their

owners, who languished in the cart while the hot rays of the sun beat down upon us.

When we reached Nimoli (now southern Sudan), I rode with a herder who had an extra camel that would take me to the Kasrashu Clan campsite.

The Kasrashu Clan was a nomadic tribe that wandered during the Monsoon seasons in search of food and grazing land. These were my mother's people. They were simple people. Tribal. When I arrived at their campsite, I noticed their resemblance to me was strong. There were 76 clansmen, women, and children. There were also 42 camels and 22 goats amongst them. For clothing, they wore layers of cloth cloaked in various ways.

They were friendly until I addressed them in Arabic. I told them that I was the son of Basamat; grandson of Majdi. No one answered. After several awkward seconds, a lone voice introduced himself in Arabic as Mansour. He was the brother to my grandfather. I asked him how it was that he knew Arabic. He replied that one couldn't barter with the traders in any other language. The Kasrashu Clan spoke only Dinka.

That night, there was a clan gathering and welcoming meal in

my honour. The Kasrashu Clan
showed their love for me. They
treated me as a distant relative
who had found his way home.
Gifts, song, food, and drink were
presented to me by the elder
women of the Clan. I found their
loving embraces, visions and
smells much like my mother's. I
missed her but felt her presence
among them. I felt more at ease
during the meal.

During the festivities, I caught the
attention of a young man whose
eyes were like black pearls. The
young man boldly approached me
and told me that he was my
cousin Kadaru. I saw a strange
resemblance to Mohammad in
Kadaru - or was it an illusion?

His smile and interest revealed much as he led me away for the night, and it was in his tent that I slept. It was customary that the day's clothing become your evening blankets. Nomadic tribes were always efficient that way. Kadaru turned to embrace me. His smell was foul but my lonesome body welcomed his advances. All the anguish and all the tiredness of the long journey drained in a compassionate sexual encounter that made me almost euphoric. When it was over, Kadaru and I lay side by side. I stroked his shoulder and arm. He whispered in broken Arabic that he loved me. Although I was euphoric and feeling thankful to Kadaru, I knew he didn't understand the significance of his words. I changed the subject. I asked him how he knew Arabic. He replied that he picked it up from the traders. He admitted that his knowledge of the language was poor but that he wanted to learn more. I didn't know if that was an invitation to me. As he went to stroke my chest his hand fell on the scroll tucked under my covers. I felt embarrassed. My mind brought up visions of Mohammad. Kadaru opened it. He turned to poem #10 and began to read. His reading was poor. His voice hoarse. His reading broke my euphoric spell. His voice, tone, and inflections hurt me like daggers. It wasn't Mohammad. It disturbed me. It wasn't the context of the poem; it was him, this place, its people. It was the wrong voice and I was far away from anything that I felt comfort for or with. I needed Mohammad.

I tore the book from his hands while he was reading. The rejection insulted him. Kadaru struck me in anger. I found myself outside his tent with all my belongings being thrown at me. I collected what I could, dressed, and started walking - without a word. I said goodbye to no one. It was nighttime but I was sure that I was heading in the correct direction towards the Nile. I was angry. I didn't know why, but I hated everything in human existence. I hated Nubia, Egypt and all the people I had encountered until then.

I sat quiet throughout the entire journey home. I found a river barge and sat among its load, steering at night while the sole boatsman slept. As on the journey there, I slept but little. I didn't clean or eat. I drank only water. The lack of food made me delirious. My arrival at the port of Asyut was unwelcomed. From the threshold of our doorway, Mohammaded looked up in horror at my disheveled appearance. He hardly recognized me. I told him everything about my horrible journey. Despite my protest, he undressed me, bathed me, and put me to bed after giving me some soup. Mohammad was leaving the room with the filthy clothes from my journey as I told him that I wanted to leave Egypt. He returned with the scroll in his hands - the scroll he had given me. "Where would we go?" he replied. His answer, his soft voice, changed my mood. I realized that Mohammad had taken care of me from the moment I entered our home, which he had never done before. I stared in awe. In Arabic I said, "Mohammad, I love you." With those words, I felt faint. I felt my body collapse from fatigue. I thought myself lucky that I was already lying in bed. Mohammad

lay down next to me and untied
the ribbon of the scroll and read
me a poem. Ironically, it was
poem number 10. As he read, my
memories of my cousin Kadaru
flashed before me. I turned to
Mohammad's vision next to me
and his words drifted away as his
soft voice put me into a much
needed sleep.

The Thin Line

Our platoon was in a company
stationed far off in the Nahre-
Saraj Desert of Afghanistan . The
squad was a rough group of thugs
and rednecks, though given the
diversity of the group, a soldier' s
neck could have been any variety
of colours despite some rather
narrow world views. Somewhere
along the way, I found myself in
charge of this gang of misfits.
"Oh hell, they all too damn stupid
to get anywhere without someone
with some brain cells between the
ears to sort 'em out'" the Captain
informed me one day in his thick
southern drawl between the
endless cigarettes he consumed
through each day. Unfortunately

it wasn't relayed as a change in rank, but more an order to watch out for the others, the same way a parent asks the oldest sibling to watch over the other kids. I learned to oversee them, reporting the sergeant when call out was done.

The guys seemed to mostly accept me. I had my chance to prove myself during initiation when they beat the crap out of me. I didn't flinch or whine or show any visible signs of being in pain. I knew if I was going to have any chance of being accepted and respected by them I would have to get past the screaming pain and mounting bruises and put on my best poker face. It was during initiation that the nicknames started to appear. I was expecting mine to be something like "Breezer" because I was short and scrawny. Thanks to my cold faced initiation experience, they instead opted to name me "Reader" after my main past time at the base. While they would be hanging out, playing cards, wrestling and smoking cigarettes, I usually had my head buried into a book. It was a convenient excuse to avoid the usual rough housing that went on between them.

In our squad, there was "Mazer" (because he walked around the beds like a maze to kill time),

"Maskow" (that was his last name), "Stone" (he was build like a brick house), Jetta (because he had pictures of VWs everywhere), myself, "Streamer" (because he pee'd for long times causing running streams on the desert sand) and "Crawl" (because of the weird way he wrestled).

"Stone" was the guy, in our company, they all were in awe of. He stood 6'4 towering over everyone. All his clothes seemed to fit his muscular form like they were almost about to rip at the seams. Once Mazer was measuring his bicep muscle and out of curiosity asked to his bicep size. Stone didn't know so they measure it. Mazer's 14 inch arms looked like twigs in comparison to 24in biceps that Stone had. Stone's skin complexion was naturally dark which was odd given his anglo heritage. His eyes were a piercing blue and how his brows rested above them gave him a scary eagle like stare. No one could take him down. Wrestling match after match, he was unbeatable. He got sick of them trying and he gradually developed an attitude of being invincible defied anyone to challenge his physical prowess.

Over time, this jovial group became more sadistic in their challenges. It was a dog eat dog world and the fighting intensified as a pecking order developed, and occasionally was challenged. There was never any doubt as to who was top dog. Having established his superiority early on, Stone took no part in fighting with the underlings. With no interest in trying to change my rank, I also stuck to my books and avoided the tides of conflicts as they ebbed and flowed with the excesses of testosterone present in group.

On occasion, I would be comfortably reading, lost in the words when a massive shape would approach me, nearly blocking out daylight streaming in through the window. "Whatcha reading now?" Stone would ask. Without any trace of sarcasm, he

would ask with keen interest
about the latest book I was
devouring. He would grow wide
eyed and I would get glimpses
into a curious little boy, the one
that existed long before he had to
put on a cloak of toughness to
survive. The normal hard edged
frown on his face would come
down, but usually reappeared as
quickly as it had disappeared.

Our Captain only came in once a
week and stayed overnight. The
company was spread so far apart
that is all time he could allow. We
knew when he was coming and
when he was going. The time in-
between was pure anarchy. If it
wasn't for the blaring heat , we
probably would have killed each

other from the boredom. Instead, during the peak heat of the day, it was usually five shirtless men smoking cigarettes and playing cards. Tempers simmering until the sun went down and any lingering resentments would be solved with fists.

The weekly Captain's visit brought with it relief supplies, mail, and always two new recruits, to relieve two of our own from field duty. They were usually from other squad stations on the parameter. This was also when new books I requested from the Military Library would arrive to me.

The letters and packages provided a brief distraction from our boredom and lethargy, but more often than not would leave us feeling more remote and isolated, longing for the loved ones who wrote us or shipped a few welcome treats.

Part of the weekly routine also included Stone checking in with which new books I had received. I could sense an urge to use the books as vehicle for discussion for us. To debate ideas and hopes and wishes, but knew his macho role would prevent him from doing so. I didn't push it, answering his questions, leaving the door open to more, for which we never got much further than a title and perfunctory explanation of the contents.

The latest two recruits arriving with the Captain were "Stretch" and "The Kid", from a squad stationed not far from us. They would replace "Streamer" and "Jetta" and of course all of the usual status battles would come to the fore. Though based on their last rotation, it didn't sound like the new arrivals would have a hard time holding their own.

The Kid starting telling us of a game called Blood, "It's a fight where everyone places a bet. You wear your t-shirt and fight until the first opponent draws enough blood from the other to write his name on the losers shirt." The victorious winner would then go on to pick their next challenger. There was also a reward, consisting of money, cigarettes and hard to find items from care packages, which grew with each match, providing a rather larger jackpot for the final winner. Mazer and Maskow were the first to bring Blood to our group. It was set for after supper that evening.

Always confident in knowing he was the toughest of the bunch, Stone skipped the scheming and planning outside and was on his way the radio room when he passed me reading on my cot. We exchanged our usual set of questions about what books I had received that week. I was about to lower my eyes back down to the page, when I blurted out "What kind of books do you like Stone?". It was a moment of impulse, words that escaped my lips before I could realize I was breaking the long standing unspoken protocol that had developed between us. Thankfully, the question didn't seem to phase him. A trace of a grin stretched across his usual tough-guy face "Me? I'm not what you call an avid reader. Get my adventures from watching movies - action and thrillers is what grabs me" It seemed like the beginning of the conversation I had been dying to have since I we first started our exchanges. Yet, given I that had already broken our unwritten rules, I thought I better not push it any further. "Oh yeah..." I said casually as I forced my eyes back down to the page. I sensed he wanted to talk some more, but even if it were the case it was all to awkward and he turned and headed for the door.

It was later that evening that Stone again reached out to me. I had just finished my kitchen clean up duty, washing the dishes, cleaning the counters and getting everything put away and ready to do it all again the next day. Stone was signing in on the log sheet at the back of the kitchen and getting ready to start his night patrol duties. A duty for which was an exercise in being busy more than it was in being safe. We were miles away from any suspected any areas of conflict, that was left to the other units. "You know, I get bored out of my skull doing the rounds on patrol. Why don't you come join me and tell me more about your books. It'll help me pass the time"

Pleased, but trying not to appear too eager, I created just a hint of doubt. "Oh, well I don't have a gun with me and I don't want to hold you up..." He looked at me rolling his eyes, "Well at the risk leaving the company wide open to enemy attack, we'll stop by the munitions house and grab you one." I had never felt so accepted and like one of the cool kids in my whole time there. Having some distance, away from the other soldiers seemed to provide Stone the space he needed to be able to open up and let down some of his toughness.

"You don't seem to hate it here like the others. I think as long as you can read you'd be happy just about anywhere" Stone said, staring off into the distance

Puzzled by this perspective, I stopped and turned to him "I hate it here. I only joined to get my school paid for. I'm counting down the days until this mission is done."

Stone's eyes narrowed, for a moment I thought he was about to put me back in line for not being one of the team. His shoulders slumped a little. "Yeah, well least you have options. The military was the only way out for me. Was never afraid of dying on the battlefield, because where I come from it was already a different kind of war zone, with drugs and gangs"

He went on to tell me his life story. He grew up in inner city Chicago. His parents split up with he was 3 years old and his mother's new man made it clear

that Stone was to be out of the
house by age 18. To make
matters worse, they lived in the
worst part of chicago. He fought
with drug dealers, his mom's
boyfriend, school kids, anyone
that wanted something from him.
Unlike the guys here that fought
to look macho, Stone had fought
for his life and his safety. He was
a skilled fighter, because his very
survival depended on it. The
invincible brick house was now
confiding in me and showing a
very uncharacteristic level of
vulnerability.

Wanting to provide some sort of
comfort to him, after sharing such
a personal part of himself, I found
myself reaching an arm around

him. "I'm sorry that you had all those things happen to you..." He didn't pull away, but I could feel his spine starting to stiffen and the elements of his familiar bravado starting to reappear.

"We'd better head back" he said having regained full control of himself again. We turned and walked back to camp in awkward silence.

When we returned the fights had already started.

Mazer kept swinging out, aiming for a direct hit at Maskow's nose, but Maskow was quick to block it. Finally, Maskow landed a good clip, right on Mazer's ear such that it started to bleed badly, and creating the first win of the night.

Subsequent matches saw Maskow challenge and be defeated by Stretch who managed to launch a fountain of blood from Maskow's split lip. Stretch wasn't so lucky with The Kid, who used his youthful speed to duck and dodge Stretch's jabs. Seizing the perfect moment, The Kid landed a right hook and down went Stretch. It seemed that the winner kept changing with each new challenger as the pot continued to grow.

When it came time for the Kid to choose a challenger he looked around the group, and suddenly his eyes locked on to me. I want to fight "Reader" he said with a cruel smile. "Me?" I sputtered? "Sorry man, I'm not part of the game, I'm not playing blood" The Kid looked like I had just slapped him. "Oh we're all playing here. It's not optional. You can't say no to my challenge". This brought a round of nods and agreement from the group. A bead of sweat began tracing its way across my forehead.

"Drop it guys" said Stone, making it clear it wasn't up for discussion. "I'm not playing your stupid game and Reader doesn't have to either" The Kid was about to say something but the threatening looks from the others convinced him it might be best to keep his mouth shut. "Alright, never mind then...Crawl, you man enough to fight me, then?" Quick to take up the challenge Crawl shot back "Fight you? I'm going to mop the floor with you!"

Content that the situation was properly diffused, Stone headed back out on his patrols and The Kid and Crawler started sizing each other up. Crawler was able to get in a few good shots, but when he was least expecting it, the Kid shot straight at his nose, and the rush of blood that began pooling on the ground was evidence of the Kid's win.

"Looks like you get the bounty tonight Kid, you've now beat everyone" Mazer said, icepack on his ear. "Not everyone" said the Kid as he spun around and again fixed his gaze on me. "C'mon Reader, let me know I won this one fair and square"

Panic started to descend over me. "It's all yours Kid, i don't want to fight you". I started to back away, heading for the safety of the barracks and my books. The Kid grabbed me by the shoulder and spun me around. He shoved me. "C'mon, fight me! At least try a little so I don't have to take away your books..." He swung a few punches my way, a good distance from my face made to provoke me more than to make any kind of contact. I felt my pulse race with fear. I knew I had to try, to run away at this point would have ruined me and left me open to future daily abuse by all the members of the company.

I aimed a few punches toward the Kid all of which he easily ducked. He taunted me a little more and I was about to land good punch on his left cheek. Unfortunately I didn't see his own fist headed for my jaw. Instantly it felt as if a cement block had struck me, pushing my teeth right through my cheek. My mouth felt like ground meat and the taste of blood was quickly overwhelming

my tongue. I spat out a mouthful.
"Think it's enough to write my
name with boys?" A few
awkward smiles momentarily
appeared, but they were quickly
replaced with wide eyes and a
look of fear.

"Tell me you weren't just stupid
enough to do what I think you
did" Stone's voice boomed out. In
record speed Stone lifted up the
Kid by his shirt collar, propped
him up against the side of the
barracks and punched him twice.
Once squarely in the eye, and the
next right in the mouth.

"Games are over for tonight boys.
I suggest you go get yourselves
cleaned up and ready for

tomorrow morning when the Captain is back". Pleased for any excuse to slip away unscathed from Stone's wrath, the rest of the group quickly slipped away and out of sight.

Stone then turned to me and I thought I was going to get a thrashing too. However, his look was more of concern. As I was starting to regain some feeling in my mouth, Stone reached out one of his large rough hands to help me up. "Let's have a look at the damage" he said His thumb and forefinger on my chin sent and arc of electricity through my body. "I'm sorry those guys did that to you" he said. I started to say something "I, I..." not sure what I wanted to say or tell him. The events quickly began to overwhelm me, tears welled up in my eyes and threatened to spill out. I turned away, embarrassed.

Sensing my vulnerability this time, Stone slipped an arm around me. "Hey, hey...it's all going to be okay now" I turned back looking at him for a second and then burying my face into his strong shoulder. He wrapped his arms around me. Gently he lifted my face. Tears streaming down my face, he looked deeply into my eyes. His stare was intense. As he gazed upon me, a single tear ran down his face as he said "You know, Reader, I really should have done this along time ago but

I didn't have the nerve." With that, he hugged me and held me tight in his arms.